Power Play

5

j   Christopher, Matthew F
           Power play, by Matt Christopher.
       Illus. by Ray Burns.   c1976.
                    4.95
                    75-33125

9-76   1.Basketball--Stories. I.Title.

Power Play

by
MATT CHRISTOPHER

Illustrated by
RAY BURNS

Little, Brown and Company
BOSTON   TORONTO

FIRST EDITION

T 08/76

Library of Congress Cataloging in Publication Data

Christopher, Matthew F
    Power play.

    SUMMARY: A magic candy bar improves Rabbit's basketball game more than is really desirable.
    [1. Basketball — Fiction] I. Title.
PZ 7. C458Po   [Fic]   75-33125
ISBN 0-316-14015-5

*Published simultaneously in Canada
by Little, Brown & Company (Canada) Limited*

PRINTED IN THE UNITED STATES OF AMERICA

Power Play

"Tough luck, Rabbit!" shouted a fan as
the ball missed the basket by inches.
"What you need is go power!"

7

Rabbit blushed. He wished he was as
tall as his brother Bones. He would
show that smart-mouth fan *then*.

Bones caught the rebound, jumped,
and made the basket.

Beetles 13, Flyers 10.

In the second quarter Rabbit caught a pass from Doc Fiddler, the Beetles' left forward. He dribbled toward the basket, then tried a jump shot.

Thump! Moonie Gordon, the Flyers' center, bumped his arm.

"Two shots!" cried the ref.

"Show us what you can do now, Rabbit!" the same fan shouted.

Rabbit badly wanted to win the fan's approval as he stepped to the free-throw line. He bounced the ball a couple of times, then shot. The ball sank through the net without touching the rim.

"Yay!" the fan shouted. "Do it again, Rabbit!"

Rabbit did.

A thunder of applause exploded
from the other Beetles' fans.

Bones smiled at him. "Man, when you hit, the fans let you know about it, don't they?"

Rabbit smiled back, feeling pleased that he had scored. "They just want to show their appreciation," he said.

The Beetles were ahead for most of the game, but in the fourth quarter the

Flyers came back and scored four baskets in a row. The score was now 38 to 36, Flyers' favor.

Then Rabbit dumped in a shot from the right corner. Next he missed an easy lay-up.

"Get a ladder, Rabbit!" yelled the smart-mouth fan again.

Furious, Rabbit looked at the crowd.
But, in that sea of faces, it was next to
impossible to find anyone yelling at
him.

Finally the Beetles won, 51 to 43.
Even so, Rabbit wasn't happy. He felt
he was the poorest player on the team
for sure. Even poorer than Nutsy Malone,
who substituted for him once in a while.

He walked home alone after the
game. Bones was ahead of him with
Rico, Chet, and Nutsy.

Why wasn't he born to be as tall
as Bones? Or why wasn't he real good

16

at something — like dribbling, or
shooting?

He had wished for months that he
would become a good basketball
player. Nothing else really mattered.

Suddenly an object on the sidewalk caught his eye. It was a bar of candy, still wrapped up in a brown, shiny wrapper.

He picked it up. CHOCO-POWER PLUS, he read. He had never seen a bar like it before.

"Eat Choco-Power Plus and feel the difference," read the small print. *"Take one bite and feel a tingle. Eat it all up and feel the POWER that will last for days!"*

Rabbit turned the bar over. The wrapper wasn't even loose. It looked safe to eat.

The thought of sinking his teeth into the candy made his mouth water. But

who had dropped it, anyway? One of
the guys with Bones?

"Hey, you guys!" he yelled, lifting
up the bar. "Did one of you drop this
bar of candy?"

They stopped, glanced back, looked
at each other, and looked back again.
"It doesn't belong to any of us!" Rico
shouted, and they went on.

Grinning happily, Rabbit removed the wrapper, stuck the bar into his mouth, and bit off a chunk. Mmm! Was it delicious! And, almost immediately, he really did begin to feel a tingle!

The more he ate, the stronger he felt it. He believed the candy was doing everything its label said it would!

The next basketball game came around almost before Rabbit realized it. It was against the Swallows.

Rabbit's pulse quickened as he watched the ref toss the ball up between the two centers, Bones and Andy Snyder.

Andy outjumped Bones, tapping the ball to Nick Taggart. But Rabbit, moving like a flash, got to the ball and grabbed it away from Nick so fast that Nick blinked. Then Rabbit dribbled it down the sideline, stopped, dodged his

guard, and shot. The ball rippled through
the net!

"Now you're cooking, Rabbit!" a
voice shouted at him from the crowd.
"Show 'em how to play the game,
Rabbit, old kid!"

Rabbit showed 'em. He plunked in
five lay-ups and four set shots in the
first quarter, and six lay-ups and five

set shots in the second. He strutted off
the court at half time feeling very
pleased with himself.

"I can't believe it!" Bones exclaimed
in the locker room. "You're playing
like a whiz, Rabbit!"

Coach Spinner smiled. "He's been
holding back on us. Keep it up, Rabbit,
and you'll be better than Bones!"

Rabbit sat proudly on the bench, a
mile-wide grin on his face. "Know

what?" he said. "I'm going to be the best. The greatest. You won't have to put in a sub for me again, Coach. I'm your best player and I'll score as many points as the rest of the guys put together."

The coach's eyebrows arched. "Oh, you will?"

"Won't that be just grand," said Bones, without smiling.

The second half was a breeze for the Beetles. They scored 28 points, 15 of which Rabbit scored himself.

They won the game 81 to 57, the highest score they had tallied so far this year.

"I was pretty good out there,"
Rabbit said to Rico after the game. He
was surprised when Rico didn't reply.

Rabbit arrived home, expecting a
nice warm reception from his mom and
dad.

He didn't get it.

Disappointed, he looked at Bones. "Didn't you tell them how many points I scored?" he asked.

"No. I thought you'd be happier to tell them that yourself, Mr. Wonderful," Bones answered, and stormed out of the room.

So Rabbit told them. They looked at him as if he were making it all up. Then they smiled and hugged him. Dad said, "Well, keep up the good work, son. Just don't get so good that you forget the other players on the team, that's all."

On Friday, when Rabbit and Bones were getting ready to leave for the game against the Hurricanes, there were several kids waiting on the sidewalk.

"What are they doing out there?" Rabbit asked curiously.

"They want to walk to the game

with you," said Bones. "After all,
you're a great hero, now."

Rabbit felt a chill race up his spine. "You go by yourself, Bones," he said nervously. "I'll go out back and by way of the railroad tracks. I know I'm good, but I don't want any crowd following me."

He sneaked out the back door, ran across the yard, climbed over the fence, then ran to the railroad tracks.

He ran along them till he reached the long bridge. He knew it was dangerous to cross it, but he felt that the Choco Bar would give him power to run swiftly across before a train came along. He started to run but soon tired. He was halfway across the bridge when he thought he heard a whistle. He

paused, listening for it to sound again.

It did! A train was coming!

He tried to go faster, missed a tie, and stumbled. He got up and looked back. Where was his newfound

strength now? He heard the whistle
again, but the train wasn't in sight yet.

He hurried on, hoping to cross the
bridge before the train reached it.

He didn't.

When he heard the blast again he
looked back and saw that the train,
smoke puffing from its smokestack,
had started to cross the bridge!

He almost froze. He would never
make it to the end of the bridge. Never.

36

Then he saw a concrete abutment
that held up the tracks. There was just
room enough to lie on it — if he could
get to it in time.

Heart thumping, he hurried to it.
Stumbled. Got up. Hurried again.
Behind him the train was closing in.

He reached the abutment and
quickly clambered down to it. Then he
lay there, trembling and sweating. He
closed his eyes and covered his ears as
the train thundered by only a couple of
feet away from him.

After the train passed by he got up, his knees feeling like rubber, and walked slowly off the bridge.

Suddenly he saw, between two ties, another bar of CHOCO-POWER PLUS! Now, how did *that* get there? he asked himself. Was it just chance, or had someone put it there?

Right away he thought of the things that eating the first bar of CHOCO-POWER PLUS had done to him. Yes, it had helped him to play basketball better than anybody else. But look what *that* had done to him. It had turned him into a bragging, self-centered kid whose own brother had turned against him.

And look at what had happened to him on the bridge. He might have gotten killed!

And what had caused it all? His belief in the CHOCO-POWER PLUS candy! It had to be!

Without another thought, he picked up the new bar of candy and flung it into the river. Then he ran down the cinder bank, crossed over to a street, and headed for the school. He got there just a few minutes before the game was to start.

Quickly he put on his uniform and ran onto the court. The whistle blew.

Bones tapped the ball to Rico, and Rico
passed it to Rabbit.

"Shoot, star! Shoot!" he cried.

Rabbit didn't shoot, though. He
passed to Doc, instead. Doc shot and
scored. Later Rabbit passed the ball to
Bones, who also scored.

"Hey, man!" cried Bones. "You're your old self again! What happened to Mr. Wonderful?"

Rabbit smiled. "I threw him into the river," he said.

Books by Matt Christopher

Sports Stories

THE LUCKY BASEBALL BAT
BASEBALL PALS
BASKETBALL SPARKPLUG
TWO STRIKES ON JOHNNY
LITTLE LEFTY
TOUCHDOWN FOR TOMMY
LONG STRETCH AT FIRST BASE
BREAK FOR THE BASKET
TALL MAN IN THE PIVOT
CHALLENGE AT SECOND BASE
CRACKERJACK HALFBACK
BASEBALL FLYHAWK
SINK IT, RUSTY
CATCHER WITH A GLASS ARM
WINGMAN ON ICE
TOO HOT TO HANDLE
THE COUNTERFEIT TACKLE
THE RELUCTANT PITCHER
LONG SHOT FOR PAUL
MIRACLE AT THE PLATE
THE TEAM THAT COULDN'T LOSE
THE YEAR MOM WON THE PENNANT
THE BASKET COUNTS
HARD DRIVE TO SHORT
CATCH THAT PASS!
SHORTSTOP FROM TOKYO
LUCKY SEVEN
JOHNNY LONG LEGS
LOOK WHO'S PLAYING FIRST BASE
TOUGH TO TACKLE
THE KID WHO ONLY HIT HOMERS
FACE-OFF
MYSTERY COACH
ICE MAGIC
NO ARM IN LEFT FIELD
JINX GLOVE
FRONT COURT HEX
THE TEAM THAT STOPPED MOVING
GLUE FINGERS
THE PIGEON WITH THE TENNIS ELBOW
THE SUBMARINE PITCH
POWER PLAY

Animal Stories

DESPERATE SEARCH
STRANDED
EARTHQUAKE